# Nobody's Perfect

*by Jenny Hessell*
*Illustrated by Mandy Nelson*

HUTCHINSON

Sometimes I think grown-ups have custard for brains. You'd think after being around for so long they'd know just about everything.

But they don't.

Take my Mum, for instance.

Ever since I can remember she's been telling me about The Terrible Things That Can Happen to Careless Children.

Some of them were just your everyday sort of terrible.

Some of them were pretty scary.

And some were so spectacular that I thought Mum must have been making them up.

Anyway, by the time
I was six, I was an
expert on how to
keep a kid safe.
Thanks to my Mum,
I was ready for
anything.

And then this kid at school died.

He wasn't fooling around on the road.
He didn't stick his finger in a socket, or mix up
gunpowder in the garage.
He didn't even climb up on the furniture.

He just got sick and had to stop coming to school,
and then one day, our teacher told us that he had died

'But that's not fair,' I said when I got home to Mum. 'You didn't say it could happen like that. You never said a kid could die just doing nothing. It's not fair!'

'Let me explain,' began Mum, but I stopped her.

'I don't want you to explain,' I scowled and I pushed past her and ran outside.

I stayed outside all day.

I decided I might never speak to my Mum again.

When she came through the garden calling me, I crawled into a hole in the hedge and pretended not to hear.

It was nearly dark when I decided that Mum might get a bit scared on her own and perhaps I'd better go in after all. I was glad I did because as soon as I saw her I could tell that she was really upset. She scooped me up and hugged me tight.

But I was still angry.

'It's so dumb,' I said, 'that he could die like that — for no reason.'

'Oh there'll be a reason,' said Mum. 'It's just that we don't know what it is yet.'

'Did the doctors know?' I asked.

'Yes,' said Mum. 'I'm sure they did.'

'Well, why didn't they make him better then?'

Mum sighed. 'Almost every time we get sick,' she said, 'the doctors *can* make us better. But there are a few things — just a very few things — which they still don't know how to fix.'

'Could it happen to me?' I asked.

'Really it could happen to anyone,' said Mum, 'but it doesn't. It happens only very very occasionally.'

'Tell you what.' She took my hand. 'Right now we have to have dinner. But tomorrow we'll go and talk to your teacher about all this. She really should have explained it better, but then, nobody's perfect.'

'You can say that again,' I muttered.

'What's that?' said Mum.

'Nothing,' I answered.